THE HUTCHINSON
BOOK OF
BUNNY
TALES

TED SMART

THE HUTCHINSON BOOK OF BUNNY TALES
A HUTCHINSON BOOK 0 091 89290 2

This edition produced for the Book People Ltd,
Hall Wood Avenue, Haydock, St. Helens, WA11 9UL

This edition published 2003

1 3 5 7 9 10 8 6 4 2

RANDOM HOUSE CHILDREN'S BOOKS
61–63 Uxbridge Rd, London W5 5SA
A division of The Random House Group Ltd

RANDOM HOUSE AUSTRALIA (PTY) LTD
20 Alfred Street, Milsons Point, Sydney,
New South Wales 2061, Australia

RANDOM HOUSE NEW ZEALAND LTD
18 Poland Road, Glenfield, Auckland 10, New Zealand

RANDOM HOUSE (PTY) LTD
Endulini, 5A Jubilee Road, Parktown 2193, South Africa

THE RANDOM HOUSE GROUP Limited Reg. No. 954009
www.kidsatrandomhouse.co.uk

A CIP catalogue record for this book is available from the British Library.

Printed and bound in Singapore

CONTENTS

The Easter Bunny

Winfried Wolf and Agnès Mathieu

MANY people don't believe in the Easter Bunny. After all, rabbits don't lay eggs!

And how could a rabbit unbolt his cage and get out all by himself?

And where would he find a basket to carry all his
Easter eggs and presents?

And everyone knows that rabbits are afraid of people.
As soon as they see you in the fields, they run away as fast
as they can.

But there really is an Easter Bunny!

He's about the same size as you are, with long, pointed ears. He wears checked trousers and a blue tail coat.

And he's very brave – he travels about the countryside all by himself with his basket of eggs.

Once a fox saw him running across a meadow and hopping across a little stream.

The fox hadn't eaten in days, and a rabbit would have made him very happy indeed.

But just in time the fox saw it was the Easter Bunny.
"Sorry to have troubled you," he said.

Another time the Easter Bunny met a fierce watch-dog
on a farm. The dog was ready to attack him, but when he
saw who it was, he just wagged his tail.

So, despite a few narrow escapes, the Easter Bunny still manages to arrive safely at your front door.

But how does he get in?

He doesn't have a key!

It's easy. His ears have special tips that open any lock.

Once he's inside, the Easter Bunny hides his eggs and presents for you.

And when it's Easter morning you have exactly the right number of Easter eggs!

If you're up on Easter morning and you look out of your bedroom window, you might catch him scurrying across your garden.

That is, *if* you believe in him.

Rabbit

Alison Catley

Listen, *Rabbit*:

Do you remember spring last year,
When we were telling stories here?

And how when Mummy called me home,
You fell, and lay there all alone?

We searched the wood, we searched the park,
We searched and searched till it got dark.
We couldn't find you.

And how next day beneath the tree,
The baby foxes came to see
The funny creature sitting there
With button eyes and tufty hair,
Just waiting.

Long and lonely days went by,
The sun grew bigger in the sky,
And soon the seeds that spring had sown
Had into summer flowers grown.
Poor Rabbit.

But then those foxes came again.
Bigger now, they played a game.

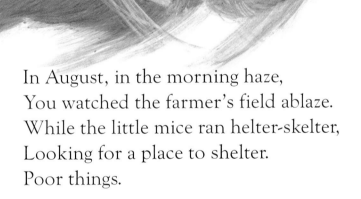

In August, in the morning haze,
You watched the farmer's field ablaze.
While the little mice ran helter-skelter,
Looking for a place to shelter.
Poor things.

The flowers died, the summer passed,
The nights were drawing in so fast.
The tree grew tired, the leaves turned brown.
The squirrels scampered up and down,
Collecting for winter.

Then there came that blustery day
When you were nearly blown away.

Listen, Rabbit, I remember
How hard it rained, that September.
You didn't have (it made me cry)
A mackintosh to keep you dry.
I hadn't forgotten you.

And when it *snowed* I couldn't rest
(You didn't have your winter vest).
The snowflakes flew and blew all over
And wrapped you in an icy cover,
While we were warm inside.

But then one fox, now fully grown,
Decided you should be at home.
Do you remember, Rabbit?

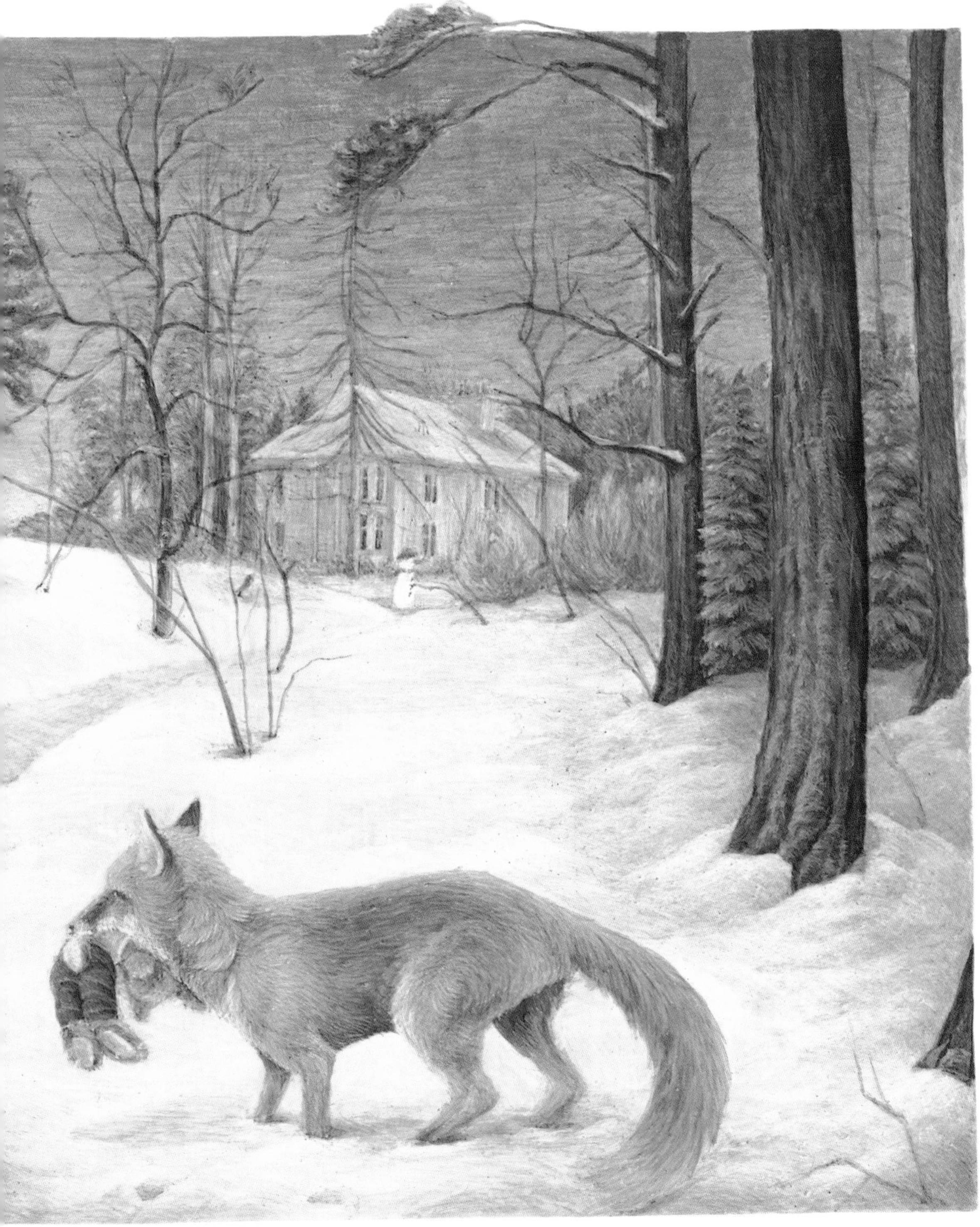

Remember how I laughed and cried
To have my rabbit safe inside.
I never will forget, you see,
The day that you came home to me.

Marmaduke
and the Scary Story

Michael Ratnett and
June Goulding

MARMADUKE, Jessica and Harriet were all very
excited. Grandma and Grandpa
were coming to stay.

"Stop fidgeting," said Dad. "Go and do something."

"Yes," said Mum. "Why not paint them a picture as a surprise?"

"Wow," said Marmaduke, as the rabbits raced up to their room. "What a great idea! I'll paint them a wonderful picture!"

"And so will I," said Jessica.

"Me too," said Harriet.

Soon they were very busy.

"No peeping!" said Marmaduke.

When they came back down, they showed each other their pictures.

Jessica had painted a picture of a butterfly . . .

Harriet had painted a picture of a flower . . .

And Marmaduke had painted a picture of a MONSTER!

"Oh Marmaduke," said Mum, "why couldn't you paint something nice like the others?"

"Pooh!" said Marmaduke. "Nice things are no fun. I like *scary* things!"

"Look what we've got for you!" said the three small rabbits as soon as Grandma and Grandpa arrived.

"Why, what lovely pictures," they said. "We can't think which one we like best!"

Then they all sat down to tea. Grandpa had *eleven* biscuits.

"Doesn't Grandpa eat a lot!" whispered Jessica.

"It's called being greedy," said Grandma.

After tea Jessica said, "Tell us a story, Grandpa."

"Of course I will," he said. "But I'll just have one more biscuit first."

"Tell them a story *now*," said Grandma. "You've had quite enough biscuits for one day."

"What sort of story would you like?" asked Grandpa.

"A SCARY story!" said Marmaduke.

So they huddled around, and Grandpa told them a scary story about a monster with three legs, just like the one in Marmaduke's picture.

"Time for bed," said Dad.

And they were monsters all the way up the stairs.

It was a dark and windy night.

"What did you think of Grandpa's story?" said Jessica.
"It was a very scary story," said Harriet.
"Yes," said Marmaduke, "but I wasn't afraid. Were you?"
"No," said Jessica.
"Of course not," said Harriet.
But they couldn't get to sleep.
Suddenly Jessica said, "W-what's that noise?"
"What noise?" said Harriet.
"Th-that's just the wind," said Marmaduke.

"Or – or a tree branch tapping," said Harriet.

They listened again.

"It's not," said Jessica. "It's coming from the stairs!"

"W-what shall we do?" said Harriet. "I'm scared!"

"One of you must go and look," said Marmaduke.

"You go and look," said Jessica. "You're the one who likes scary things!"

"All right, we'll all go together," said Marmaduke.

Shivering from the tips of their ears to the ends of their toes, they climbed out of bed and crept towards the door. Marmaduke went in front, firmly grasping his cricket bat.

When they were on the landing, they looked down. There, coming up the stairs, was a huge shadowy figure! Thump, thump, click, it went. Thump, thump, click . . .

"It's the three-legged monster!" stammered Marmaduke. And he raised his cricket bat way up high . . .

. . . and hit the monster thwack on the head!

"Ow!!" yelled Grandpa.

Then the light came on.
"What *is* all this noise?" said Dad.
"Marmaduke hit me on the head!" said Grandpa.
"We thought he was a monster!" said Marmaduke.

"Well he is *sometimes*," said Grandma, "especially when he creeps about after biscuits."

And they all laughed.

Mum made everyone a mug of steaming cocoa and sent the three small rabbits back to bed.

"I still think you were very brave, Marmaduke," said Jessica.

"I do too," said Harriet, "even though Grandpa wasn't really a monster."

But Marmaduke was busy.

"ROAR!" he screamed!

Little Rabbit's Big Day

Charlotte van Emst

It was a big day for Little Rabbit. He was going to the park with Bear.

"Be good," said Mum as she waved goodbye, "you're a big rabbit now."

"Remember, Bear," said Little Rabbit, on the way to the park, "I'm not little today. I'm *big*!

"In fact, I'll soon be too big for this pushchair."

The moment they arrived, Little Rabbit rushed straight for the swings. "Look at me!" he cried. "Big rabbits can swing *really* high."

Back and forth and up and down he went, higher and higher . . . and higher . . . and higher . . . and HIGHER . . .

"Whoops!"

When Bear looked round, Little Rabbit was already halfway up the slide.

"Look at me!" he shouted. "No hands!"

"Wheeeee!"

BUMP!

But Little Rabbit was determined to be big and brave. "Let's play hide-and-seek," he said.

Bear found a good hiding place. Little Rabbit looked over here and over there; under this and under that. He couldn't find Bear anywhere.

"Where are you?" he sniffed.

"Over here!" cried Bear, jumping out from behind a tree. "I've found *you*."

But big, bold rabbits never stay miserable for long . . .

On the way to the duck pond they watched the Teddy Rovers practising for Saturday's big match. "I'll show you how to play football," yelled Little Rabbit. "Just watch me!"

Little Rabbit gave the ball a huge kick . . .

"Ouch!"

"Well done," said the big centre forward. Little Rabbit felt very proud, even though his toe hurt quite a lot.

At last they reached the duck pond. "Those ducks look hungry," said Little Rabbit. "See how far I can throw."

The bread went soaring through the air and so did Little Rabbit.

SPLASH!

"That was a *huge* throw," said Bear, helping him out.

"I'll jump myself dry," suggested Little Rabbit. "I'm good at jumping."

But the mud was all slippery . . .

"Never mind," said Bear. "Let's have an ice cream."

Little Rabbit chose a treble decker strawberry whiz with a chocolate flake. "Big rabbits need really big ice creams," he said.

"And we can eat them all in one go!"

"I think it's time we went home," said Bear. "It's been a big day."

Back at home, Little Rabbit began to feel small again. He let Bear run his bath.

He let her rinse his face when he got soap in his eyes.

"Don't worry, you'll soon feel better," said Bear, as she wrapped him up in a nice warm towel.

Little Rabbit hoped so!

Later on, Bear was busy in the kitchen.
"There's a surprise for tea," she said.

Little Rabbit was glad he
was small enough for special
surprises . . .
like chocolate cake.

He was glad he was small enough for it not to matter too
much if he made a mess.

He was glad he was small enough to be carried upstairs and cuddled and read a story and tucked up tight and kissed goodnight.

I'm glad I'm not *always* a big rabbit, he thought as he closed his eyes.

But one day . . .

Osbert and Lucy

Ronald Ferns

SOMEWHERE in a small town there was a certain house. Mr and Mrs Good lived there with their dog, Osbert Good. In the back garden there was a little hutch where Lucy, a white rabbit, lived.

Osbert and Lucy were good friends.

Osbert Good was a very nice dog, except for one thing: he liked to listen at doorways. One day he overheard three words that made him very upset. They were: "delicious", "rabbit" and "dinner".

This could only mean one thing. No! They couldn't, they mustn't eat his friend Lucy.

Osbert hurried into the garden to tell Lucy what he had overheard. Lucy didn't like the idea of becoming dinner for Mr and Mrs Good. But Osbert had a plan. They would run away together.

In the middle of the night, Osbert opened the door to Lucy's hutch and out she hopped. She put some lettuce leaves in a tiny bag. Osbert took with him a bone and an umbrella.

They set off together into the night. Although Osbert walked slowly, Lucy had to hop very quickly to keep up.

The rain fell in big drops, making large puddles on the pavement. "Oh, what shall we do! Where shall we go!" wailed Lucy.

"Everything will be all right, as long as we stay together," said Osbert.

Soon they came to an empty house. There was a sign outside saying:

FOR SALE

"Let's rest here for a while," said Osbert.
He shook the raindrops from his umbrella while Lucy held the bags of food.

As Lucy leant against the door, it began to open. Cautiously, the two friends crept inside and bravely climbed the stairs.

"No one will find us here," said Lucy, beginning to feel better. They were both tired and hungry.

Lucy nibbled her lettuce leaves and Osbert gnawed his bone. Soon they were both fast asleep.

They woke up as the dawn sunshine shone through the dusty window. Osbert and Lucy peered out together. This was what they saw:

There was a neat garden with flower beds.

There was a vegetable patch.

There were some fruit bushes.

And beyond the gate there was a leafy wood.

They raced downstairs. The back door was locked, but at the bottom they found a cat flap. Lucy slipped through easily.

Osbert found it rather difficult, but he squeezed and he huffed and he pushed and he puffed and, eventually, he found himself outside.

"Oh it's lovely," cried Lucy, looking round the garden. Soon she was enjoying a fine breakfast of tender lettuce leaves and fresh carrots.

Poor Osbert wandered around hoping he could find something to eat. If only he were a vegetarian, too.

Then he noticed a packet near the wall. Inside were sandwiches: corned beef, cheese and jam. He was so hungry and in such a hurry to eat that he dropped most of the slices of bread.

Birds flew down from the trees and snapped up the bread. Ants scurried from the cracks in the path and carried the jammy bits away to eat at home.

Soon everything was gone, and Osbert could find nothing to eat at all.

Lucy loved life in the garden. She found plenty of carrots and lettuce leaves, but poor Osbert grew hungrier and hungrier.

He sat down in a corner of the garden and wished, "If only sausages, bones, lamb chops, and biscuits grew on trees." But they didn't.

Osbert thought about his comfortable home, his regular meals and his basket. Then he thought about his favourite ball and his collection of  squeaky toys. He became very sad and great big tears rolled down his nose. "Rabbits can live in the wild," he said sadly. "But dogs need a home, and a bone and a warm, dry basket."

He wandered off to find Lucy. She was holding hands with another rabbit. "This is Henry," she explained. "He came over from the woods where he lives. He has asked

me to marry him, and I feel like saying yes. But what will you do, Osbert?"

"Congratulations!" said Osbert. "Oh, I do hope you'll be happy. Please don't worry about me, I'll go back home. After all, I don't think they'll eat *me* for dinner."

So Lucy and Henry were married.

When Osbert reached home again, Mr and Mrs Good were very pleased to see him.

"How clever of Osbert to find our lost umbrella," they said. "What a pity he couldn't have found Lucy as well."

Later that same day, after eating a good meal of leftover chops, Osbert began listening at the door again. This time he heard the words: "delicious", "dinner" *and* "now – the dessert".

Mrs Good walked out from the kitchen carrying a large wobbly pink jelly rabbit! Osbert felt rather silly. So they hadn't meant to eat Lucy after all!

Still, he was glad he and Lucy had run away because now he could visit Lucy and Henry in the wood. They have a very large family with many children, a number of grand-children and several great-grand-children.

And Osbert knows that although he needs a home and a bone and a dry basket, Lucy is much better off where she is.

Rabbit
Gets Ready

Claire Fletcher

RABBIT WOKE UP feeling different. Today was a very special day – his first day at a new school. He was excited and happy, but he was nervous too and there was a strange feeling in his tummy. It was eight o'clock. He had to get dressed quickly if he was going to be there on time. He didn't want to walk in late with everyone looking at him – Rabbit felt quite weak at the thought.

He opened his wardrobe. He had lots of clothes; coats and trousers and shoes, and shirts and jumpers. What should he put on? Everybody else will know what to wear, thought Rabbit. It was so unfair.

He tried on his knitted swimming costume. It was great for diving and somersaulting at the pool, but not quite right for school.

Next Rabbit put on a striped jacket and a straw hat. He had spent a lovely day with Dog on the river bank eating peanut butter sandwiches and looking at the boats. Maybe . . . The jacket was smart enough, but the others were sure to laugh at him if he wore *that* hat.

What about his beloved dungarees, with safety pins where buttons should have been? He usually wore them chug-chugging along on board the big red tractor at the farm. But Rabbit threw them on the floor. Everyone would think he was a real scruff in those.

Rabbit's funny feeling was growing. All he wanted was to fit in. It was such an important day, but he just couldn't seem to make up his mind.

He unruffled his best hat, trimmed with feathers. It had been such a hit at Monkey's party. But no, thought Rabbit. He didn't want to draw *quite* that much attention to himself. Not on his first day anyway.

Rabbit frantically rummaged about. Something big and bright caught his eye. It was the jumper Aunt Maud had given him last summer. "I expect I shall be quite warm enough without *that*!" said Rabbit, scornfully.

Rabbit glanced at his watch. "Oh dear, oh dear, I'll be late if I don't find something soon," he sighed.

He spotted his blue sailor suit and tried it on. As he marched up and down with a nautical air he could almost taste the salt and hear the call of the seagulls. Rabbit was beginning to wish that *he* could run away to sea. As far as he knew, sailors didn't go to school.

Poor Rabbit. Suddenly he heard the beep beep of the school bus outside the door. There was no time to lose. Rabbit grabbed the last thing from his cupboard – his stripy football jersey. He ran out of the door as fast as he could, clutching his lunch box in his paws.

The schoolyard brimmed with all the colours of the rainbow. A group of pigs and cats were having a picnic in the middle. There was a water trough with boats and ships and there was even a tortoise on a big red tractor. Rabbit wanted to join in, but the funny feeling in his tummy was worse.

He felt very alone and just a little bit scared.

Then he saw a small bear standing timidly in the corner of the playground. He did look smart, but he didn't look very happy. Rabbit took a deep breath, marched over and took the bear by the paw. "Are you new?" said Rabbit. The bear nodded, shyly. Rabbit smiled. "Come on then," he said.

Together they ran as fast as they could to the end of the playground. "Kick it here . . ." "To me . . ." came the cries from all around. Rabbit jumped for joy – he would soon make friends. And his funny feeling had quite, quite gone. Perhaps tomorrow he would wear . . . Oh bother, thought Rabbit. Who cares . . . And he let out a shout – "Let's PLAY!"

Rabbit Magic

Susie Jenkin-Pearce and Julia Malim

NOVEMBER grey, end of day.
Mist time,
   smoke time,
     rabbit time,

magic time.

Small boy follows
through the gate. Golden
time, berry time, crimson
leaves in the lake.
Footsteps follow, join
the chase.
Where to? Where next?
Look around. What's
hiding there in the
autumn leaves and
evening light?

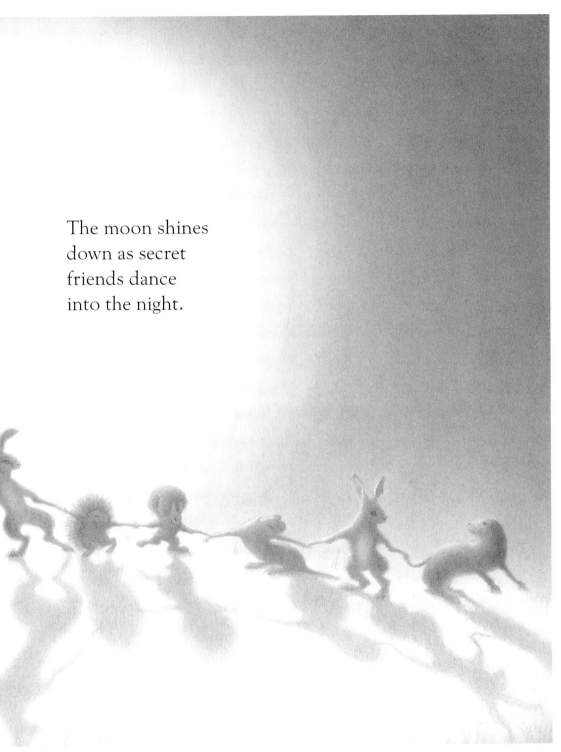

The moon shines
down as secret
friends dance
into the night.

Follow rabbit through his door, time is passing into sleep. Falling snow, winter time, peaceful snow, feather soft.

Spring sun shines and small boy wakes, follow rabbit, flutter wings. Buds unfurl and thrush sings sweet, the season's green, the blossom's pink.

Small boy follows
through the arch, to
gold and blue.
The spring has passed.
Silent heat and poppy
red, a summer's beauty
will not last.

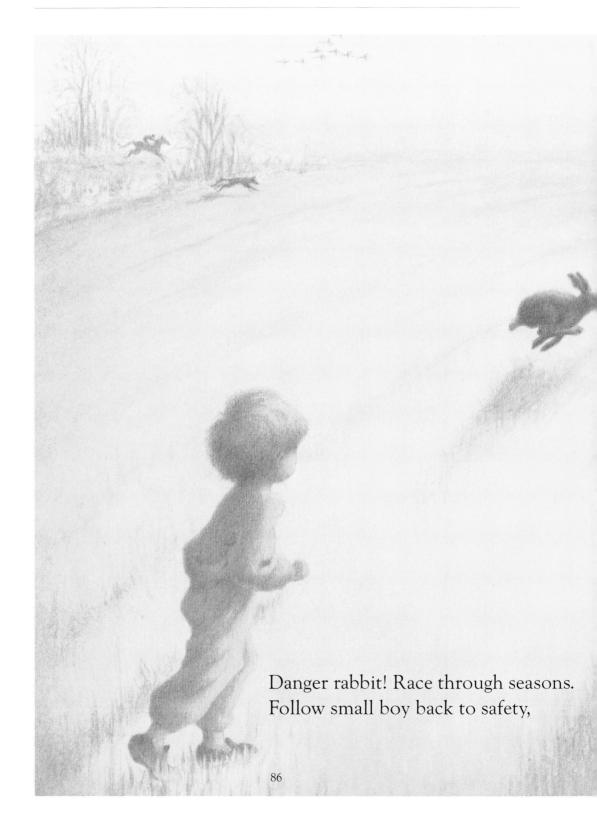

Danger rabbit! Race through seasons.
Follow small boy back to safety,

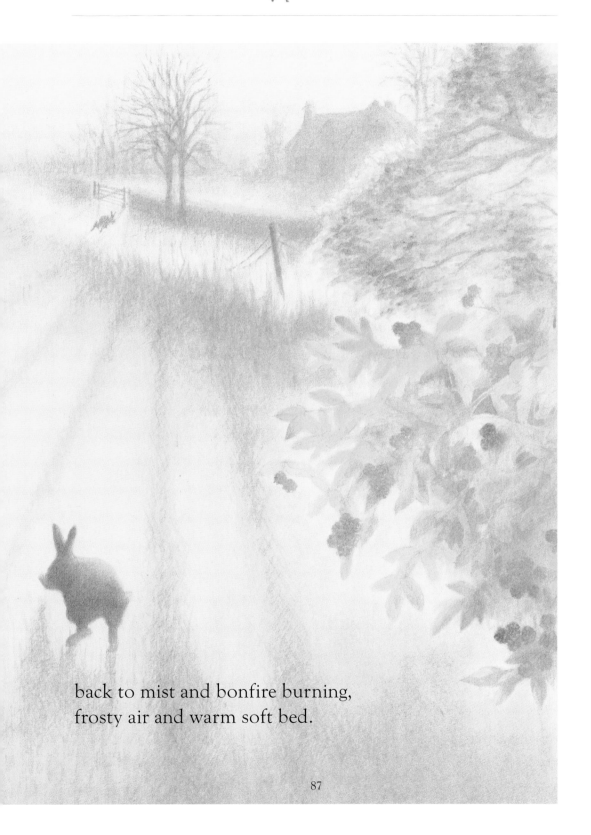

back to mist and bonfire burning,
frosty air and warm soft bed.

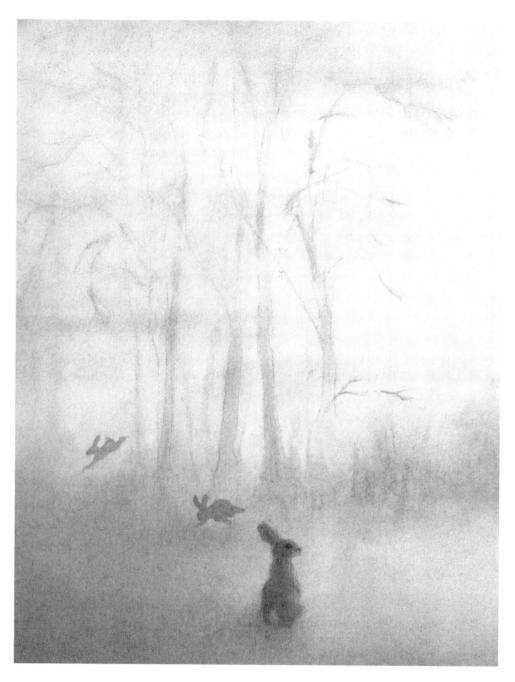

November grey, end of day. Mist time, smoke time,

rabbit time,
magic time.

Mimsey and Binks

Caroline Castle and Peter Bowman

Mimsey was a fine toy monkey with bristling brown fur and a long, long tail. He wore a smart red waistcoat and a tartan bow tie and he always looked just right.

Binks was a chattery felt rabbit who had seen better days. His ears had lost their stuffing and drooped down floppily by the side. His old dungarees were too big and the knitting had started to unravel. But Binks was full of joy and, for all his scruffiness, he was Mimsey's best friend and he loved him more than anyone in the whole wide world.

Every morning, in the time between sunrise and breakfast when toys come alive, Mimsey and Binks would take a stroll around the playroom. Mimsey would march up and down in a straight line, holding up his tail so it didn't drag on the carpet and lose its bristle.

But Binks! Oh, Binks would run and jump and tumble and bounce and somersault. And Mimsey would say, "Oh, you must be careful, Binks, you'll hurt yourself."

But Binks was so full of joy that he couldn't help it, and very soon Mimsey would be full of joy too, just watching Binks enjoy their early morning time together.

One morning Binks began to sing because it was a fine March day and he had just seen the first flowers of spring appear in the garden. At first Mimsey told him to be quiet in case he woke up the children, but the song was so jolly and funny that he was soon joining in the chorus, which went:

Springtime brings the daffodilly
Summer brings the rose and lily
Autumn brings the ripe red cherry
Winter brings the holly berry.

It was then that Mimsey saw a letter sitting on the doormat. Quickly, and with great excitement, he opened it up while Binks looked over his shoulder.

"Oh, my!" said Mimsey. "Cousin Brooster is coming to visit."

"How exciting!" said Binks, doing a somersault. "What's he like?"

Mimsey took a deep breath. "Well," he said, "he's very smart."

"Smart," said Binks gravely.

"And very big and grand and clever," continued Mimsey. "And he likes everything to be *just so.*"

"Oh, goodness," said Binks, standing on his head.

The toys were up especially early next morning to tidy the Wendy house for Brooster's visit. They polished and scrubbed and dusted and swept until everything shone.

But as Mimsey watched Binks at work something began to worry away at him; worry away and worry away until he finally said, "Dear Binks, I think you should have a new outfit for Brooster's visit."

Mimsey rummaged around in the odds and ends box until he found a smart pair of tartan trousers. They were a little tight and he squeezed and pushed and pushed and squeezed until finally Binks was inside them.

"I think they are a bit *small*," said Binks squeakily.

"But they look marvellous," said Mimsey. "Just hold your breath and pull your tummy in."

When Mimsey and Binks had finished their chores they sat down to wait for the knock on the door. Binks began to wonder what he could do to entertain their visitor.

"Shall I do some of my tricks?" he asked.

"Best not," said Mimsey. "I don't think he likes tricks."

"Best not, then," said Binks. "Well, shall I sing a song . . . or do a dance?" he added hopefully.

"Best not," said Mimsey. "I don't think he likes

singing or dancing."

"Oh, best not, then," said Binks.

Then Mimsey looked at Binks sitting quietly in the chair with his floppy ears and the same worried feeling came back.

"I tell you what!" said Mimsey suddenly. "I think you should wear a hat."

"A hat?" said Binks.

"Yes, a *hat*," said Mimsey. "You'll look very smart in a hat." And he disappeared into the dolls' house and returned with a large bobble hat with a pom-pom which he pulled tightly over Binks's ears.

"There you go, Binks, dear chap," he said. "That will keep you nice and warm."

"But I'm not *cold*," said Binks in a small voice. But Mimsey didn't hear.

Mimsey plumped up the cushions in the Wendy house and put the kettle on to boil. Then he brushed his fur and straightened his bow tie. Binks sat quietly in a corner, fidgeting uncomfortably in his smart new trousers.

Outside, the birds sang, the milk cart rattled, and the big clock tick-tick-tocked. In fact everything was as it always was in their special early morning time. But something was missing.

All Binks's joy was gone.

As Mimsey looked at Binks sitting quietly in the corner, he seemed to get smaller and smaller in his chair until he seemed nothing more than a crumpled bundle of felt and tartan.

"Oh, my goodness," sighed Mimsey. "Dear Binks. Where have you gone?"

Minutes later Binks was back inside his warm, comfortable blue dungarees and his ears once again flopped happily about as he bounced around the room. Almost at once, heavy footsteps sounded down the garden path and the doorbell rang.

Mimsey rushed to open it. There stood the biggest, furriest and most magnificent toy gorilla Binks had ever seen.

"Brooster!" cried Mimsey. "Come in, come in."

Brooster strode inside. Mimsey showed him around while Binks jumped and tumbled and bounced and sang as he set the table for tea.

The sun shone, the birds sang and the clock tick-tick-tocked, just as it always did.

"What a happy place!" exclaimed Brooster.

"That's because of my friend Binks," said Mimsey proudly.

"My very best friend in the whole wide world."

The Carrot Patch

Zoe Figg

W ARREN WAS a rabbit who belonged to himself. He was small and brown and always busy in his big garden.

If he wasn't digging, he was planting. If he wasn't planting he was watering. If he wasn't watering he was sorting out his shed or keeping an eye on the weather.

There was always such a lot to do if you were a rabbit with a garden. He belonged to himself, and didn't want any help from anyone.

One spring morning Warren felt that somehow it was a special kind of day. "Of course!" he exclaimed as he looked at his gardening calendar. "It's carrot planting day!"

Warren grew the crispiest, juiciest, sweetest, fattest carrots in the countryside.

He looked in the packet of seeds and smiled to himself. I have a feeling that this year's carrots will be the best yet!

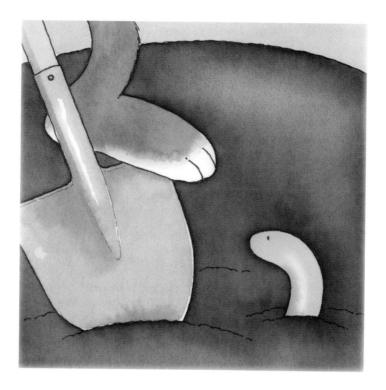

As Warren set off for the vegetable patch he imagined the splendid harvest he would have in the summer. As he started to dig he thought about all the delicious things he would cook: carrot soup, carrot pie, carrot trifle, and iced carrot cake.

After a while, Worm popped up to see what was going on. "Hello, Warren," he said brightly. "Need any help? I'm a good digger!"

"No, thank you," said Warren. "I can manage fine by myself. And anyway, you are too wriggly to dig in straight lines."

Worm wriggled off feeling a little sad.

As Warren carefully planted his seeds, some sparrows flew down. "Hello, Warren," they chirped. "Need any help?"

"No thank you, sparrows," he replied. "I can manage fine by myself. And anyway, you will probably eat my seeds!"

"Suit yourself," chirped the sparrows and they flew off, feeling rather offended.

When he had planted all his seeds, he began to stamp with his big feet to flatten the ground. After a while, Mole popped up. "Hello, Warren. Need any help?" he asked kindly.

"Thank you, Mole," replied Warren. "But I can manage fine by myself. And anyway, your paws are too tiny to be any good."

And Mole slunk away, feeling a little small.

Finally, when everything was done, Warren fetched his watering can and watered the seeds. This time, nobody offered to help and he was rather pleased. "I managed fine all on my own," he said to himself. "I don't need any help from anyone."

The months passed by. The rain came down and the sun shone.

Then one morning Warren noticed the first little carrot shoots coming up through the earth. It wasn't long before some snails came slithering by. "Hello, Warren. Need any help?" they asked.

"No I don't!" said Warren. "And don't you dare eat my seedlings!"

"Hurrumph," said the snails. "We only wanted to help. Well, as he is so rude, we *will* eat some of his nice, juicy seedlings."

And they did.

"Oh, dear," said Worm, when he saw what had happened. "Poor Warren. Only one seedling left. He's not going to have much of a harvest now."

One summer morning, Warren woke up and knew for sure that it was a special day. Carrot picking day! He hurried down to the carrot patch. "Oh, dear. Only one carrot left," he said. "But never mind, at least I've grown it all by myself." He started to pull.

"That's funny, it won't budge," he said to himself. He pulled again. The carrot still wouldn't budge. So he pulled some more, harder and harder, but still the carrot stayed firmly in the ground.

Just then, Worm popped up again. "Need any help?" he said brightly.

Warren thought for a moment. Perhaps it wasn't such a good idea trying to do everything by yourself after all.

"Yes, please, Worm," he said. "That would be very kind."

Worm burrowed around the edges of the carrot while Warren pulled. But still the carrot wouldn't budge.

Then the sparrows flew over. "Need any help?" they chirped.

"Oh, yes, please!" called Warren. "That would be very kind."

And they all began to pull. But still the carrot wouldn't budge.

Mole appeared. "Hello, Warren," he said. "I know my paws are small, but I'd be happy to help."

"Oh, Mole, thank you," said Warren. And Warren and the sparrows and Mole all began to pull. But the carrot wouldn't shift.

Finally, the cheeky snails slithered over. "We're sorry we ate your seedlings," they said. "Can we help?"

"Thank you," said Warren. "With all of us pulling together we just might do it."

And while Worm burrowed, Warren and the sparrows and Mole and the snails all pulled as hard as they could.

All of a sudden the earth began to move, they all fell over, and up it came –

The biggest,

juiciest,

sweetest,

fattest carrot that Warren

had ever grown!

Warren put the giant carrot in his wheelbarrow. "Thank you, everyone," he said. "I expect you're hungry after all that hard work. If you'll let me, I'd like to help."

"That would be very kind," said Mole.

Back at his house, Warren cooked a great feast of carrot soup, carrot pie, carrot bread and iced carrot cake for everyone.

Warren looked at his new friends. "Thank you," he said. "It's good to do things on your own. But it's much nicer doing things together."

Carrot Tops and Cottontails

Jan Mark and Tony Ross

Here is a tale of long ago, in the days when
vegetables could talk. None of you has ever heard a
vegetable talk. This is why.

Once upon a time in a green and pleasant valley, there was a hedge. On one side of the hedge lay a field, and in the field lived a colony of peaceable rabbits.

On the other side of the hedge was a garden. In the garden lived a band of gallant carrots.

At morning and evening the rabbits came out of their burrows and nibbled the grass, and the grass never complained, for the rabbits kept its hair tidy. Under the ground it was busy being grass roots, discussing important matters. Like many clever persons, the grass would never have bothered to get its hair cut – had it not been for the rabbits.

In the mornings the carrots lay in bed with only the plumes on their hats showing, but in the evenings they rose up and basked in the glow of the setting sun. Carrots always look their best at sunset, and these were very vain carrots.

Unlike the grass, the carrots never said anything important. They were too busy admiring themselves and showing off before the other vegetables, the lettuces who were fat and vulgar, the cabbages who had big hearts but

no brains, the turnips who were dull and earthy, and the radishes, who were insignificant.

The only things that did not admire the carrots were the rabbits. They were occupied on the far side of the hedge, eating grass, and anyway, they had been taught that it is rude to stare.

The carrots were affronted. They posed, they preened, they twirled the feathers on their hats until even the beetroot turned pale with envy, but the rabbits just went on eating grass.

In the end the carrots could bear it no longer.

"I say!" they shouted. "I say! You there, with the silly ears!"

"Us?" said the friendly rabbits, and they hopped to the hedge where the carrots were jeering in a row.

"Yes, you," said the carrots. "I say, you, *why* do you have such silly ears?"

The rabbits were hurt.

"We do not think our ears are silly," they said. "And they are the only ears we have."

"And silly or not," said the eldest rabbit, "with our ears we can hear our friend the grass."

"Why listen to grass when you could listen to us?" the carrots bawled, but the rabbits turned away and went back to the field. They were very loyal.

The next evening the carrots were there again, flouncing and flaunting while the other vegetables stood in line to admire them.

"I say!" shouted the carrots. "I say! You there, with the silly tails!"

"Us?" said the courteous rabbits, and they hurried to the hedge.

"Yes, you," said the carrots. "I say, you, *why* do you have such silly tails?"

The rabbits were offended. "We do not think our tails are silly," they said. "And they are the only tails we have."

"And silly or not," said the youngest rabbit, "when one of us turns up his tail and runs, we know that danger is near."

They turned their backs and hopped away.

The arrogant carrots saw their bobbing tails and fell about, laughing.

The next evening the carrots were lying in wait for the rabbits, and when the rabbits came out they began to hoot and hiss.

"I say, I say!" the carrots called. "You there, with the silly eyes!"

"Us?" said the patient rabbits, and they hastened to the hedge.

"Yes, you!" said the carrots. "I say, you. *Why* do you

have such silly eyes?"

The rabbits were incensed. "We do not think our eyes are silly," they said. "And they are the only eyes we have."

"And silly or not," said the fattest rabbit, "we can see what happens behind us without turning our heads."

They went back to their field without turning their heads to look at the barracking carrots.

"But we can still see you," said the fattest rabbit.

The next evening, when the rabbits came out, the carrots were there in a row by the hedge.

And they all shouted, "I say! I say! You there with the silly teeth!"

"Us?" said the angry rabbits and they hurtled to the hedge.

"Yes, you," cried the carrots. "I say, you, *why* do you have such silly teeth?"

The rabbits were outraged. "We do not think our teeth are silly," they said. "And they are the only teeth we have."

"And silly or not," said the toughest rabbit, "our teeth will bite through anything."

"*Anything?*" sneered the carrots. "Could they bite through a tree? Could they bite through a stone? Could they bite through a brick?"

"No no no," said all the rabbits together. "But they could bite through *you.*"

And then the rabbits thundered under the hedge and fell upon the carrots. The carnage was frightful. Not a carrot remained alive, for though they were rude and fearless, they could not withstand the teeth of the vengeful rabbits.

And when the carrots were slain, the rabbits turned upon the radishes and the beetroots, the cabbages and lettuces and the earthy turnips who had gathered round to watch. When night fell, the garden was laid waste.

And since that time no carrot has been safe in the presence of a hostile rabbit, and all other vegetables fear their terrible teeth. But the rabbits still live in peace and harmony with grass, coming out of their burrows at morning and evening, to trim its hair, while underground the grass roots continue to discuss important matters, and

sometimes people ask their opinion.

But no one speaks to vegetables, and vegetables do not speak at all. They dare not.

I once heard of a small farm in Connecticut where on autumn evenings the pumpkins can be heard singing "God Bless America".

But that was told to me by a seafaring sheep with one eye.

He may have been lying.

Acknowledgements

The publishers gratefully acknowledge the following authors and illustrators:

The Easter Bunny/Der Osterhase: Agnès Mathieu and Winfried Wolf
© by Ravensburger Buchverlag Otto Maier GmbH, Ravensburg (Germany), 1984

Rabbit published by Hutchinson Children's Books
© Alison Catley, 1991

Marmaduke and the Scary Story published by Hutchinson Children's Books
text © Michael Ratnett, 1990; illustrations © June Goulding, 1990

Little Rabbit's Big Day published by Hutchinson Children's Books
© Charlotte van Emst, 1989

Osbert and Lucy published by Hutchinson Children's Books
© Ronald Ferns, 1988

Rabbit Gets Ready published by The Bodley Head Children's Books
© Claire Fletcher, 1995

Rabbit Magic published by The Bodley Head Children's Books
text © Susie Jenkin-Pearce, 1993; illustrations © Julia Malim,1993

Mimsey and Binks
text © Caroline Castle, 2003; illustrations © Peter Bowman, 2003

The Carrot Patch
© Zoe Figg, 2003

Carrot Tops and Cottontails published by the Andersen Press
text © Jan Mark, 1993; illustrations © Tony Ross, 1993